COLLECTED WORKS

RECENT RESEARCHES IN THE MUSIC OF THE BAROQUE ERA

Christoph Wolff, general editor

A-R Editions, Inc., publishes seven series of musicological editions
that present music brought to light in the course of current research:

Recent Researches in the Music of the Middle Ages and Early Renaissance
Charles M. Atkinson, general editor

Recent Researches in the Music of the Renaissance
James Haar, general editor

Recent Researches in the Music of the Baroque Era
Christoph Wolff, general editor

Recent Researches in the Music of the Classical Era
Eugene K. Wolf, general editor

Recent Researches in the Music of the Nineteenth and Early Twentieth Centuries
Rufus Hallmark and D. Kern Holoman, general editors

Recent Researches in American Music
H. Wiley Hitchcock, general editor

Recent Researches in the Oral Traditions of Music
Philip V. Bohlman, general editor

Each *Recent Researches* edition is devoted to works
by a single composer or to a single genre of composition.
The contents are chosen for their potential interest to scholars
and performers, then prepared for publication according to the
standards that govern the making of all reliable historical editions.

Subscribers to any of these series, as well as patrons of subscribing institutions,
are invited to apply for information about the ''Copyright-Sharing Policy''
of A-R Editions, Inc., under which policy any part of an edition
may be reproduced free of charge for study or performance.

For information contact

A-R Editions, Inc.
801 Deming Way
Madison, Wisconsin 53717

(608) 836-9000

RECENT RESEARCHES IN THE MUSIC OF THE BAROQUE ERA • VOLUME 66

Henry Butler

COLLECTED WORKS

Edited by Elizabeth V. Phillips
with Basso Continuo Realizations and
Commentary by Jack Ashworth

 A-R Editions, Inc.
Madison

Performance parts are available from the publisher.

Library of Congress Cataloging-in-Publication Data

Butler, Henry, d. 1652.
    [Works. 1991]
    Collected works / Henry Butler ; edited by Elizabeth V. Phillips ;
with basso continuo realizations and commentary by Jack Ashworth.
    1 score. — (Recent researches in the music of the Baroque Era,
ISSN 0484-0828 ; v. 66)
    Divisions on a ground (13 sets) for viola da gamba and continuo; 2
preludes for viola da gamba and continuo; 1 sonata for viola da
gamba and continuo; 1 aria for violin, viola da gamba, and continuo;
and 3 sonatas for violin, viola da gamba, and continuo.
    Unfigured bass in 14 compositions; figured bass in 6 compositions.
    Includes bibliographical references.
    1. Variations (Viola da gamba and continuo)—Scores.   2. Viola da
gamba and continuo music—Scores.   3. Sonatas (Viola da gamba and
continuo)—Scores.   4. Trio sonatas (Violin, viola da gamba,
continuo)—Scores.   5. Improvisation (Music)   I. Phillips,
Elizabeth V.   II. Ashworth, Jack.   III. Series
M2.R238   vol. 66
[M3]   91-751062
ISBN 0-89579-263-X   CIP
                                                    M

Contents

Preface

Introduction

This edition of Henry Butler's works expands the available repertory of early seventeenth-century instrumental music, particularly music for the bass viol (viola da gamba). The twenty pieces that can be attributed with reasonable certainty to Butler, mostly divisions on grounds for bass viol, also include music for one or two string instruments with basso continuo. These works appear in ten manuscript sources.

Despite the small number of surviving works by Butler, his music is important both stylistically and historically. The culmination of the English virtuoso division repertory for bass viol may be seen in Butler's contributions to the genre, which exhibit unusual length, variety, and technical difficulty. In contrast, his works for violin, bass viol, and continuo display both English and Italian style characteristics. The pairing of violin and viol shows English influence, as does the use of chordal viol writing within that combination. The Italian concept of sonata is seen in the titles, structures, and stylistic features of these works. Butler's single extended work for bass viol and continuo (no. 16 in the edition) may be the earliest composition to apply sonata style to that performing medium. Certainly Butler was among the first English-born composers to experiment with the sonata. Historians of early seventeenth-century music will also note Butler's unique position as an English musician working in Spain.

The Composer

Henry Butler, alias Don Enrico Butler (d. 1652), was recognized in the seventeenth century as a composer of exemplary divisions on grounds for the bass viol and as a virtuoso performer on that instrument. He spent the years from 1623 until his death as a member of the musical establishment at the court of Philip IV of Spain.[1] Information about Butler comes primarily from Spanish court documents: the notice of his initial appointment, which states that he was a native of Sussex; a notice of appointment to the rank of *gentilhombre de casa,* in 1637; payroll accounts; and various memoranda.[2]

Butler's skill as a performer impressed his contemporaries, as evidenced by the following statement from James Wadsworth (the younger): "Moreover there is one M. *Henry Butler,* which teacheth his Catholike Maiesty to play on the Violl, a man very fantasticall, but one who hath his pension truely payd him for his fingers sake."[3] The composer Andrea Falconieri honored Butler in the dedication of a pair of pieces published in 1650, "Canciona dicha la preciosa, echa para Don Enrico Butler" and "Su gallarda."[4] And a few years after But-

ler's death, his music was praised by Christopher Simpson, the foremost authority on divisions for the viol: "I would have you peruse the *Divisions* which other men have made opon *Grounds;* as those of Mr. *Henry Butler,* Mr. *Daniel Norcome,* and divers other Excellent Men of this our Nation, . . . Noting in their *Divisions,* what you find best worthy to be imitated."[5] The final tribute to Butler appeared in 1687, when Jean Rousseau cited him and three others as English viol-playing composers who brought a chordal style of playing to courts on the Continent.[6]

Research in England and Spain has revealed no information about Henry Butler's date of birth, family, musical training, or reasons for going to Spain. Several persons named Henry Butler are cited in seventeenth-century English documents, but none of them can be identified with certainty as the composer.

The Music

Butler's compositions are all instrumental. The majority belong to the genre of divisions on grounds for bass viol, with implied basso continuo accompaniment. Two preludes (nos. 7 and 9 in the edition) and an untitled work (no. 16) are written in two parts, clearly intended for bass viol and continuo. Three sonatas (nos. 18–20) and an aria (no. 17) require violin, bass viol, and continuo.

When and where Butler composed his music is not known. Nor is there evidence of other works by him that have not survived.[7] Stylistic considerations and the fact that Simpson knew Butler's divisions suggest that these works and their preludes originated in England. The Italianate characteristics of numbers 16, 18, 19, and 20 could reflect Butler's stay in Rome (1644–?1647) or his interaction with Italian musicians who served with him in the Spanish Capilla Real and perhaps acquainted him with the sonata repertory.

THE DIVISIONS

The art of improvising or composing divisions on grounds for the viol was cultivated in seventeenth-century England. Simpson's tutor *The Division-Violist* provides both instructions for improvising and examples of composed divisions.[8] English manuscripts contain more than one hundred sets of viol divisions—many anonymous and most by little-known composers—that display stylistic features also seen in Simpson's divisions.

Divisions by Butler[9] appear in four of the ten sources of his music. (Most of these manuscripts probably originated in the late seventeenth century, the rest in the early eighteenth century. On the sources of Butler's music, see The Edition, under "Sources.") As a whole, his works stand apart by virtue of their demands on the viol player. Some of Butler's sets contain many more than the genre's typical five to fourteen divisions; numbers 1 and 4, respectively, include forty-nine and thirty-seven divisions. The wide range, up to four octaves, sometimes requires tuning the lowest string from D to C, as does certain other English viol literature. On the highest string Butler's music requires playing far beyond the frets, occasionally up to c'''. Furthermore, the player must execute double stops in the highest register, sometimes in conjunction with rapid passagework or wide leaps. Such technical demands call for a virtuoso performer.

Apart from their unusual length and difficulty, Butler's divisions display most conventions of the genre. Several sets are based on grounds related to common ground bass types: *romanesca* (nos. 1 and 12), *folia* (nos. 5, 8, and 15), *passamezzo antico* (no. 14), and *passacaglia* (no. 4). The ground of number 13 is associated with a common harmonization of the broadside tune "Callino casturame"; the tune itself appears at measure 106.[10] Each division introduces one or two "points of division"[11] (melodic-rhythmic motives used in sequences) to break up the notes of the ground or to create counterpoint against the ground. Although Butler's harmonic procedures are not unusual for his time, some of his divisions exhibit more harmonic variety and dissonances than do viol divisions by many other composers.

Set 8 bears attribution to "Sēgr. Jon." (Young?) in one of its two sources (see Critical Notes below). The present edition credits the work to Butler on the basis of its stylistic similarity to other divisions by the composer, the reliability of the concordant (and principal) source, the location of the work amid a large group of pieces by Butler in the source that names "Jon.," and the pairing in that source of number 7 (the prelude to no. 8) with another composition by Butler (no. 16 in the present edition; see plate 1).

THE PRELUDES

Preludes precede sets of divisions (nos. 8 and 10) in two sources. Because of the way the pairs are arranged on the page and because a single key governs each pair, it appears that the composer or copyists intended for the prelude to introduce the divisions in performance. As noted above, the E-minor prelude (no. 7) is placed directly before the E-minor sonata (no. 16) in one source, and not before set 8, also in E minor; this placement could be a copyist's error. The paucity of prelude-divisions or prelude-sonata combinations in early seventeenth-century viol repertory[12] suggests that such pairings were not common practice. Their presence in two separate sources shows Butler's possible interest in multimovement genres, if indeed he was responsible for the pairings.

THE SOLO SONATA

The sonata-like piece for viol and continuo (no. 16) likewise reflects a multisectional approach to formal organization.[13] Like sonatas for solo instrument and basso continuo by Biagio Marini, Dario Castello, Giovanni Battista Fontana, and others, this work consists of several distinct sections differentiated by meter, texture, and melodic material. Although the unique source of number 16 fails to provide a title or to identify the solo instrument, musical characteristics relate the piece most closely to Italian sonatas of Butler's time and limit performance of the solo part to the bass viol. The solo part contains multiple stops that can be executed only on the bass viol or a plucked instrument, and the latter can be ruled out because of the use of staff notation rather than tablature, among other reasons. Virtuoso viol writing and abundant sequences link this work stylistically to Butler's divisions. Its continuo part is unfigured, as in his other viol music but not as in his works involving violin.

A few collections printed during Butler's lifetime contain sonata-like works for a bass-range instrument and continuo: canzonas by Girolamo Frescobaldi (1628), fantasias by Bartolomeo Selma y Salaverde (1638), and sonatas by Giovanni Antonio Bertoli (1645). While some of these works specify "fagotto," the others apparently leave the choice of instrument to the performer; none is technically restricted to the viol. Thus Butler's sonata-like piece may be the earliest known example of that genre exclusively for viol and continuo, predating the first printed viol sonatas (Johannes Schenck, op. 2, 1688) by more than thirty-five years. Since it also preceded the solo sonata of Henry Purcell (for violin and continuo, n.d.)[14] and the earliest sonatas of Daniel Purcell (three each for violin and recorder, with continuo, 1698), Butler's composition could be the first sonata-like work for solo instrument and continuo written by an English composer.

THE ENSEMBLE ARIA AND SONATAS

The instrumental combination of violin, bass viol, and continuo was particularly favored by English composers. In addition to the aria and three sonatas credited to Butler, works by William Young,[15] John Jenkins, and Poole[16] call for this combination. In their compositions the bass viol part generally functions in *concertante* fashion, not merely doubling the continuo. Jenkins, John Coprario, William Lawes, Christopher Gibbons, and others left "setts" (now commonly called fantasia-suites) for violin, bass viol, and organ.[17] This English genre was made up of a fantasia movement, an almaine or ayre, and a galliard, corant, or sarabande. The inclusion of a written-out organ part instead of figured bass differentiates nearly all of this repertory from Butler's works. Most of the composers named were skilled viol players, and they frequently made greater technical demands on the viol player than on the violinist.

The Aria for violin, viol, and continuo (no. 17) resembles the ayre or almaine found as the middle movement of English fantasia-suites. Most such instrumental ayres, like Butler's Aria, are in duple meter and consist of two strains. Moreover, the title Aria connects this work to Italian instrumental arias of the seventeenth century, some of which likewise exhibit duple meter and two-part form. The possibility exists that Butler's piece once belonged to a fantasia-suite or other multimovement composition.

Three sonatas for violin, viol, and continuo (nos. 18–20) are attributed to Butler, although number 20 bears the name "Zamponi" in one source.[18] These works contain several sections contrasting in texture and melodic material. Imitative and homophonic textures alternate, melodic sequences abound, and motives are occasionally extended by means of Fortspinnung. Italian tempo indications (presto, adagio, allegro) mark changes of tempo within each work. The uncontested sonatas (nos. 18 and 19) share many features. Both are in major keys, both include dancelike sections of triple meter, and both incorporate numerous double stops in the viol part. Sonata number 20 remains in a minor key and duple meter throughout and contains no double stops. Furthermore, it is unique in displaying a passage of imitation (mm. 46–66) between continuo and strings, and another passage with rhythmic augmentation (mm. 90–110). Despite these obvious differences, which might suggest a different composer for number 20, the G-minor sonata does bear further resemblances to numbers 18 and 19. Particularly striking is the pattern of successive solos in numbers 19 and 20, where each of the string instruments has passages with the basso continuo alone. The two sonatas also contain considerable chromatic inflection in sequences.

As indicated by most of the stylistic features just described, Butler's sonatas resemble Italian sonatas from the first half of the seventeenth century. But whereas many of these Italian compositions call for violin, a *concertante* bass instrument, and continuo, the specified bass instruments (e.g., *trombone, fagotto, violetta, violone*) do not include viol.[19] In the second half of the century, sonatas for violin, viol, and continuo were written by Austrian and German composers, including Johann Heinrich Schmelzer, Johann Philipp Krieger, Philipp Heinrich Erlebach, and Dietrich Buxtehude. Several theories have developed concerning the transmission of sonata styles among English, Italian, and German composers.[20]

Butler's role in the development of the sonata for violin, viol, and continuo remains conjectural. Certainly he was among the earliest English-born composers of that genre. Except for the designation "Fantasia" in one source, "Sonata" is the only title applied to numbers 18–20. These pieces combine an English instrumentation and the English style of bass viol writing with an Italian approach to structure and with the more Continental figured bass, used in place of a fully composed, English-style organ part.

Notes on Performance

INSTRUMENTS

The standard English bass viol of Butler's day had six strings, commonly tuned D–G–c–e–a–d'. Division sets 1 and 2 include low Cs, requiring the lowest string to be tuned to that pitch. An unusual tuning is probably not required for numbers 9 and 10, despite two five-note chords that are virtually unplayable as written in their sources, using standard tuning (no. 9, m. 10, and no. 10, m. 104). Transmission of scribal errors from an earlier source to the surviving manuscripts is a more likely explanation than the need to retune the G string to F.[21] The edition adds a sixth note to each chord, so that both can be played in standard tuning relatively easily.

Although the manuscript pages of Butler's divisions and preludes name no instrument, circumstantial evidence points to the bass viol. The viol parts of numbers 18–20 variously refer to "viol de gamba," "viola di gamba," "Viola di G.," or simply "viola." As in numbers 1–17, the nature of the music mandates the bass viol.

Violin parts in numbers 18–20 are most often labeled "violino," but one source (Durham, Cathedral, Dean and Chapter Library [hereafter GB:DRc], Mus MS. D.2) uses "violi" and "viol.," perhaps as abbreviations. The unspecified treble part of number 17 appears in sources for numbers 18–20 and resembles their violin parts in range and character.

Basso continuo instruments are discussed in the Commentary on the Basso Continuo Realizations. None of Butler's pieces specifies the continuo instrument, but two manuscripts that include his music (GB:DRc, Mus MS. D.10, and Brussels, Bibliothèque du Conservatoire Royal de Musique, MS. Litt. XY, no. 24.910) refer elsewhere to "organ," "organo," "teorbano," and "harpsecord."

TEMPO INDICATIONS

Only three of Butler's compositions (nos. 18–20) contain tempo indications, all Italian terms. In early seventeenth-century music, allegro means both "fast" and "cheerful," adagio both "slow" and "contemplative."[22] Presto at that time could mean *tempo giusto*, contrasting with adagio; sometimes used interchangeably with allegro, as in number 18, presto is another way of saying "quick."[23]

ORNAMENTATION

Ornament signs appear in the manuscripts of numbers 17 and 19. The principal source exhibits *tr*; a second source, *tr* or *//*; and the third source, +. Seemingly equivalent in their use, these signs occur over a single note or centered above a group of slurred thirty-second notes. The meaning of these ornaments is not entirely clear. The sign *tr* might stand for the Italian *trillo* or *tremolo* or *tremoletto*. It is probably not an abbreviation for *trill*, since the English used the term *shake* for a rapid alternation of adjacent tones, like the Italian *groppo*.[24]

By the time Butler's works were copied into the extant sources, it is conceivable that *tr*, *//* , and + had become generic signs for any suitable ornament. Which if any of these signs Butler himself wrote remains unknown, along with the intended interpretation. Even more enigmatic is the matter of adding ornamentation not indicated by signs. An argument can be made that divisions are per se ornaments to a ground. But a division incorporating long notes, such as division 14 of number 2 or division 1 of number 13, may tempt a performer to improvise, perhaps in the expressive manner of the Italian aria rather than in the more mechanical division style. Certainly the compositional style of numbers 16–20 offers opportunities for cadential formulas and other appropriate ornamentation.

The Edition

SOURCES

The music included in the present edition comes from ten manuscripts.[25] Ten of Butler's works are preserved as unica; the others are found in from two to eight sources. All the manuscripts probably date from after Butler's death. Although the origins and scribes of these sources are unknown, three manuscripts are bound into copies of Simpson's division viol books, and names of possible owners appear in two sources. Eight of the manuscripts contain music by both English and Continental composers, some from the late seventeenth century.[26] A listing of all known sources and the sigla by which they are identified in the Preface follows:

B:Bc (Brussels, Bibliothèque du Conservatoire Royal de Musique), MS. Litt. XY, no. 24.910. Three partbooks. (No. 18)

GB:DRc (Durham, Cathedral, Dean and Chapter Library), Mus MS. D.2. Three partbooks. (Nos. 17–20)

GB:DRc, Mus MS. D.5. Three partbooks. (Nos. 18–20)

GB:DRc, Mus MS. D.10. Oblong score format. (Nos. 1, 2, 4, 5, 7–20)

GB:HAdolmetsch (Haslemere, Carl Dolmetsch, private collection), MS. II.C.25. Three partbooks. (No. 18)

GB:Lcm (London, Library of the Royal College of Music), II.F.10(2.). Manuscript bound into Simpson (1659).[27] (Nos. 3, 6)

GB:Lgc (London, Gresham College, Guildhall Library), Gresham Mus. MS. 369. (Nos. 18, 20, violin parts only)

GB:Ob (Oxford, Bodleian Library), MS. Mus. Sch. C.71. Manuscript bound into Simpson (1667). (No. 14, complete; no. 18, viol part only)

GB:Ob, MS. Mus. Sch. D.249. Three parts. (No. 18)

US:NYp (New York Public Library, Lincoln Center), Drexel 3551. Manuscript bound into Simpson (1659). (Nos. 2, 7–10, 14)

The principal source for most of the divisions is GB:DRc, Mus MS. D.10, the unique source of numbers 1, 4, 5, 11–13, 15, and 16. Because this manuscript contains many errors and some unusual features, the alternative source of numbers 2 and 7–10—US:NYp, Drexel 3551—is preferable. For number 14 the most complete source is GB:Ob, MS. Mus. Sch. C.71. Several sources of number 18 provide clear readings, including GB:DRc, Mus MS. D.2, the manuscript selected as principal source. Overall, this manuscript seems more reliable than GB:DRc, Mus MSS. D.5 and D.10, and it provides consistency for all the works involving violin, viol, and continuo (nos. 17–20).

At least a few errors appear in each source. Copyists' mistakes are not surprising, especially in the divisions, since manuscripts probably circulated among amateurs;[28] six extant copies of Simpson's viol treatise contain bound-in pages of manuscript divisions, and Simpson himself noted the prohibitive expense of publishing divisions.[29] Concordances have provided some assistance in correcting obvious errors, but editorial judgment was sometimes required for interpreting a source or deliberately departing from it. All editorial changes are indicated in the score or Critical Notes.

EDITORIAL METHODS

The numbering of works in the edition is editorial and corresponds to that in Gordon Dodd's *Thematic Index of Music for Viols* (London: Viola da Gamba Society, 1980–89).[30] Most titles shown in this edition are also editorial. These appear in square brackets; information about the few original titles is supplied in the Critical Notes under "Source(s)." Editorial titles provide key designations for convenience, notwithstanding certain modal characteristics found particularly in the divisions. Regarding the bracketed names of instruments supplied on the opening page of each piece in this edition, see Notes on Performance.

In the sources viol divisions on grounds normally were written on single five-line staves, with frequent clef changes to avoid the use of ledger lines. (This typical format is followed in the supplementary viol performance part to the present edition.) The ground was usually written only once, at the beginning. Simpson's recommendation that the viol play the initial statement of the ground unaccompanied[31] is reflected in the edited full scores. The manuscripts provide no further continuo grounds, except for a few reiterations in GB:DRc, Mus MS. D.10, an unusual example of score notation. Grounds are repeated editorially, and the placement of the ground in the source is reported in the Critical Notes. In numbers 1–16 of the present edition, the full score places the viol part on a grand staff, for ease of reading. Original clefs are not cited. In the viol parts of numbers 17–20, clef changes are inconsistent among the sources and have been resolved editorially without report. Clefs in the supplementary viol performance part are mostly editorial and have been limited to three kinds: bass, alto, and treble. For the basso continuo parts of numbers 16–20, differences in clefs between the edition and principal source are described in the Critical Notes. Where clef signs seem to be missing in the sources but are assumed editorially, the putative clef change is reported.

All basso continuo realizations are editorial. Information about continuo performance may be found in the Commentary on the Basso Continuo Realizations. Figured bass numerals and accidentals duplicate those of the principal source, unless cited otherwise in the Critical Notes. Figures have been placed below the staff, rather than in their original location above the staff, and they have been tacitly aligned editorially. The edition retains original sharps and flats in the figures; natural signs have not been substituted.

Most meter signatures are original; exceptions are bracketed in the edition if added editorially or cited in the Critical Notes if emended. Editorial suggestions for proportional relationships accompany changes of meter and appear above the staff. The edition tacitly changes the meter and rhythm of a ground where necessary to conform to a particular division. Barlines have been regularized editorially but generally correspond to those of the sources. Some double barlines are editorial, separating divisions or distinct sections of a work. Numbering of individual divisions on a ground occurs in some sources and has been used throughout by the editor, who is also responsible for applying the letters *A* and *B* to the strains of two-part grounds. (Thus "B3" designates the third division on the second strain of the ground.)

Note values in the edition are those of the principal source. However, where a source contains unstemmed noteheads having less than a whole-note value as the inner notes of viol chords, the edition tacitly adopts one of the outer note values of the chord. (In actual performance only the highest note or two of a chord can be sustained, and no standard notation precisely represents the sound of three-to-six-note multiple stops played on a viol.) The edition tacitly reduces the number of stems in some multiple stops. Coloration (blackened semibreves), used briefly in numbers 1 and 4, is mentioned in the Critical Notes, as is the white notation (open-headed eighth and sixteenth notes) in a section of number 16. The editor has substituted beamed notes for some original groups of flagged notes; tied notes for some dotted notes, breves, and notes that extend across a barline; and dotted notes or single notes for some tied notes—all without comment. Other editorial ties appear as dashed curves. Some beamed notes have been regrouped.

Tempo indications shown in numbers 18–20 appear in at least one source but rarely in all three parts, and not always at the same measure. Their appearance in the source(s) is described in the Critical Notes and their placement regularized in the edition. Concordant sources vary somewhat in the use and location of tempo indications and the term *solo*. The editor has placed each tempo term at the beginning of a section.

Ornament signs (*tr*) shown in numbers 17 and 19 are original, but their placement in the principal source is imprecise, and their appearance varies among concordant sources. Slurs are original unless dashed. Deleted or emended slurs are accounted for in the Critical Notes.

In the sources an accidental may appear before, above, or even below the note it inflects and applies only to that note and, in some instances, to immediate reiterations of that note. The placement of accidentals has been modernized in the edition, and the status of an accidental (that is to say, source or editorial) remains in force throughout the measure unless canceled or changed; redundant signs have been tacitly deleted. Thus within a single measure reiterated pitches separated by intervening notes and rests may be inflected alternately by source and editorial accidentals (see, for example, no. 14, m. 20). Purely editorial accidentals are enclosed in square brackets. A canceling accidental not signaled in the source but implied by source procedures and required as a consequence of modern convention appears in parentheses. (The modern natural sign substitutes for an original sharp or flat for cancelation.) Editorial cautionary accidentals are shown as smaller-size accidentals.

The edition provides a uniform key signature throughout each piece, although one may be lacking in part or all of the principal source. Places where a key signature is missing are reported in the Critical Notes. Only in number 16 does the lack of a key signature in some sections suggest a deliberate change of harmonic orientation by the composer. For this piece the editor has supplied a single key signature but in certain measures has canceled its effect by means of bracketed accidentals.

Notes and rests in brackets have been supplied by the editor. Emended pitches and other data supplied by concordant sources are described in the Critical Notes along with other editorial corrections and some significant variant readings. Brackets also enclose editorially supplied fermatas and numerals indicating triplets or other groupettes. Redundant groupette numerals have been omitted tacitly.

In the manuscript sources a fermata and/or a double barline with pairs of double dots appears at the conclusion of many sections of some works. The editor has placed final fermatas on final notes, including fermatas located over the concluding double barline in the sources. A double barline with a pair of dots (modern repeat sign) in a set of divisions seems to signal the end of a division rather than a need for repetition. The same sign, found in some sources of numbers 17 and 18, may indicate repetition. The edition omits the sign, but the Critical Notes report its occurrences.

Critical Notes

The critical notes for each piece cite all known sources (for source abbreviations, see The Edition under "Sources"). If more than one source is listed, the first one is the principal source used for the edition. The identification of sources also includes information about original titles, if any, and attributions.

All reports refer to the full score and describe discrepancies between the edition and the principal source of each work unless otherwise indicated. The separate bass viol performance part duplicates the pitches of the viol parts in the scores but places the music on a single staff to aid the performer.

Each entry supplies as much of the following information as necessary: the measure number(s), the part(s), the staff, the number(s) of the note(s) on that staff, and the comment. Critical notes for numbers 1–16 refer to the bass viol part unless otherwise indicated. The following abbreviations are used: M(m). = measure(s), U = upper staff of viol part, L = lower staff of viol part, bc = basso continuo, v = viol, vn = violin, and div(s). = division(s). Single notes and vertical sonorities (double stops or chords) both count as one note; tied notes count as two notes; rests are counted separately. Reference to a change of pitch implies the same duration if no difference is mentioned. Pitch designations show c'–b' as the octave above middle C, c–b as the octave below that, and so forth. Short-title citations to modern editions of Butler's works are to the following studies:

Erslev, Wendy. "Divisions to a Ground (*Drexel 3551*): An Edition and Commentary." Master's thesis, Brooklyn College, 1977.

Gutmann, Veronika. *Die Improvisation auf der Viola da gamba in England im 17. Jahrhundert und ihre Wurzeln im 16. Jahrhundert.* Wiener Veröffentlichungen zur Musikwissenschaft, vol. 19. Tutzing: Hans Schneider, 1979.

Richards, Janet. "A Study of Music for Bass Viol Written in England in the Seventeenth Century." 3 vols. B.Litt. thesis, University of Oxford, 1961.

1. [DIVISIONS IN C MAJOR]

Source

GB:DRc, Mus MS. D.10, 116–24: "H:B:"

Edition

Richards, "Music for Bass Viol" 2:153–57.

Notes

Lowest string must be tuned to C. Ground appears on a separate staff below divs. 1 and 21 only. M. 1, numeral 2 in meter signature appears superimposed on a numeral 1. M. 8, L, note 2, c is half note. M. 53, L, note is e and lacks dot. M. 54, L, note 2 is three-note chord c–g–c'. M. 68, L, notes 1–4 are sixteenth notes. Mm. 76–96, half notes are indicated by blackened semibreves (coloration). M. 80, U, notes 1–4 have additional slur. M. 83, notes 1–2 have additional slur, notes 4–6, slur is over notes 4–5 only. M. 84, second slur possibly includes note 8. M. 86, first slur is over notes 1–3, second slur is over notes 6–8. M. 97, meter signature is $\frac{3}{2}$, with numeral 2 superimposed on a numeral 1. M. 131, notes 4–5 have slur. M. 139, U, note 4 is possibly c'. M. 147, note 12 appears to be c". M. 151,

L, note 7, a is half note slurred to f eighth note. Mm. 159–60, edition assumes alto clef. M. 163, note 1, edition assumes alto clef. M. 172, L, note 2 is followed by extraneous half note c. M. 177, notes 4–7 are eighth notes. M. 197, L, note 1 is eighth note. M. 200, L, notes 1–3, and U, notes 1–4, edition assumes alto clef.

2. [DIVISIONS IN C MAJOR]

Sources

1. US:NYp, Drexel 3551, MS, 16–19: "Mr Buttler."
2. GB:DRc, Mus MS. D.10, 124–28: "H:B."

Editions

Erslev, "Divisions," 136–46; Gutmann, *Die Improvisation*, app., 9–11—both editions based on source 1.

Notes

Lowest string must be tuned to C. Ground appears before div. 1 only; source 2 is in score format. A fermata appears at the end of each strain. M. 36, L, notes 11–12 have slur in source 2. M. 47, U, note 6 is f♯'—edition follows source 2. M. 55, note 5, chord also includes f dotted quarter note in both sources. M. 64, L, notes 1–4 are eighth notes and notes 5–6 are quarter notes in source 1, notes 5–6 are quarter note (C) in source 2. M. 79, L, notes 4–5 have slur in source 2. M. 81, notes 9–10 are eighth notes—edition follows source 2. M. 87, note 14 is eighth note—edition follows source 2. M. 90, U, notes 5–6 have slur in source 2. M. 98, notes 2–3 have slur in source 2. M. 100, L, notes 1–2 have slur in source 2. M. 103, L, note 3 is eighth note—edition follows source 2. M. 110, notes 8–15 have slur in source 2. M. 112, L, note 17 is half note—edition follows source 2. M. 128, U, notes 1–3 and 12–14 are sixteenth note and two thirty-second notes—edition follows source 2.

3. [DIVISIONS IN C MAJOR]

Source

GB:Lcm, II.F.10(2.), 4v–5r: "In C"; "Mr Butler:"

Notes

Ground A appears before div. A1 only; ground B appears after div. A1 only. Some strains end with :‖: . M. 12, note 2, edition assumes bass clef. M. 14, L, note 4 lacks dot. M. 24, note has fermata. M. 26, notes 1–3 are sixteenth notes. M. 32, note 7 has fermata. M. 44, notes 14 and 15, separated by extraneous thirty-second notes (b, a). M. 49, meter signature is $\frac{3}{1}$. M. 70, U, notes 3–5 are e', f', g'. M. 72, U, note 6 has fermata.

4. [DIVISIONS IN D MAJOR]

Source

GB:DRc, Mus MS. D.10, 129–31: "H: Botler:"

Edition

Gutmann, *Die Improvisation,* app., 12–13.

Notes

Ground appears on a separate staff below divs. 1 and 13 only. M. 46, note 1, blackened semibreves (coloration). M. 103, note 1 is c♯'. M. 148, U, notes 2–4 are f♯', e', d'. M. 149, note 2, c♯' lacks stem. M. 153, U and L, breve.

5. [Divisions in D Minor]

Source

GB:DRc, Mus MS. D.10, 132–38: "H:B:"

Notes

Ground appears on a separate staff below divs. 1 and 10 only. M. 20, U, note 3 is three-note chord c"–e"–g", note 4 is double stop b'–d". M. 21, U, note 1 is c". M. 32, L, note 1, f♯ is quarter note, chord is c–e–f♯–a. M. 39, U, note 1, and L, note 8, edition assumes alto clef. M. 40, L, notes 1–2 have slur. M. 47, L, note 1 is eighth note; U, notes 5–7 are g', a', b♯', notes 8–15 are c", b♯', c", b♯', c", b♯', a', b'. M. 48, U, note is b'. M. 52, U and L, note 1, edition assumes alto clef. M. 55, U, notes 5–7, edition assumes soprano clef. M. 56, U, note 1 edition assumes soprano clef. M. 104, U, notes 1–4, edition assumes soprano clef. M. 123, L, note 1, edition assumes bass clef. M. 144, U, note 5, d' and f♯' lack dots. M. 145, meter signature is ₵. M. 156, note 8 is b. M. 159, U, note 1, g' lacks dot; L, note is b. M. 160, U, note 5, and L, edition assumes alto clef. M. 162, note 18, sharp is placed before note 19. M. 163, note 3, sharp is placed before note 2. M. 172, U, note 9 is eighth note.

6. [Divisions in D Minor]

Source

GB:Lcm, II.F.10(2.), 12v–13r: "In D"; "M Butler" (fol. 12v), "Mr Butller" (fol. 13r)

Notes

Ground A appears before div. A1 only; ground B appears after div. A1 only. Fermatas or repeat signs (:‖:) or both appear at the end of most strains. M. 15, note 8 is g'. M. 26, L, note 12, sharp is placed below note 11. M. 30, L, notes 6–9 are sixteenth notes. M. 31, U, notes 3–6 are sixteenth notes. M. 32, U, note 8 has superfluous sharp below note. M. 33, meter signature is ₃⁄₁. M. 34, L, note 3 is f. M. 35, note 1 is c'. M. 36, note 9 lacks dots. M. 40, note 8 lacks dot. M. 48, U, note 10 has superfluous sharp above note. M. 49, L, notes 2, 4, 6, and 8 have superfluous sharps apparently pertaining to notes 3, 5, and 7. M. 50, U, note 3, sharp is placed above note 4.

7. [Prelude in E Minor]

Sources

1. US:NYp, Drexel 3551, MS, 37
2. GB:DRc, Mus MS. D.10, 160: "Prel"

Edition

Erslev, "Divisions," 195 (based on source 1).

Notes

Basso continuo part precedes viol part; source 2 is in score format. Key signature of F-sharp is missing in source 1, which signs each F individually, except where noted below (e.g., "note 3 lacks sharp"); edition follows source 2, which has a signature of F-sharp. M. 7, U, note 3 lacks sharp. M. 10, L, note 1 has sharp on d in source 2. M. 11, L, note 3 is a♮—edition follows source 2. M. 12, L, note 3 lacks sharp. M. 13, L, note 1 lacks sharp on f.

8. [Divisions in E Minor]

Sources

1. US:NYp, Drexel 3551, MS, 37–39: "Mr Buttler."
2. GB:DRc, Mus MS. D.10, 139–42: "Sēgr. Jon."

Editions

Erslev, "Divisions," 196–205 (based on source 1); Gutmann, *Die Improvisation,* app., 14–16 (based on source 2); Richards, "Music for Bass Viol" 2:182–83 (based on source 2).

Notes

Grounds A and B appear before div. A1 only. Source 2 is in score format. Order of divs. follows source 1; source 2 has A, A1–6, B, B1–6. A fermata appears at the end of each strain. Key signature of F-sharp is missing for mm. 8–19 (note 5) and 21–26 (note 7); source 1 signs each F individually in these measures, except where reported below (e.g., "note 3 lacks sharp"). The editorial meter signature is added after source 2. M. 18, L, note 5 lacks sharp. M. 19, note 7, d' is quarter note—edition follows source 2. M. 23, U, note 2 has sharp in both sources; L, note 6 has sharp in source 2. M. 26, note 3 lacks sharp and is double stop e–f—edition follows source 2. M. 29, U, notes 4–5 have slur in source 2; L, note 1 has sharp on d in source 2. M. 30, U, note 4, value is unclear—edition follows source 2. M. 45, L, notes 2 and 4 have sharp in source 2. M. 48, L, note 1, g is eighth note—edition follows source 2. M. 52, U, note 5, f♯' is sixteenth note—edition follows source 2. M. 65, note 4 has sharp on c' in source 2. M. 69, U, note 3, b is eighth note, note 9, a' is eighth note—edition follows source 2 in both cases. M. 71, U, note 7 has sharp in source 2. M. 75, U, note 1 is sixteenth note, note 2 is whole note—edition follows source 2; L, notes 1–3 are sixteenth notes—edition follows source

2—notes 2 and 4 have sharp on g in source 2. M. 77, U, note 1 lacks one dot—edition follows source 2. M. 89, U, note 4 has sharp in source 2.

9. [PRELUDE IN F MAJOR]

Sources

1. US:NYp, Drexel 3551, MS, 30
2. GB:DRc, Mus MS. D.10, 143: "Prelut:"

Edition

Erslev, "Divisions," 178 (based on source 1)

Notes

Basso continuo part precedes viol part; source 2 is in score format. M. 1, slur appears to be under either notes 1–3 or 1–4—edition follows source 2. M. 10, L, editorial note is added to make multiple stop playable in standard tuning (see also no. 10, m. 104).

10. [DIVISIONS IN F MAJOR]

Sources

1. US:NYp, Drexel 3551, MS, 30–33: "Mr Butler."
2. GB:DRc, Mus MS. D.10, 143–48: "Cront." (143), "H: B:" (145), "Henrich Botler." (145), "H. B." (148)

Edition

Erslev, "Divisions," 179–89 (based on source 1).

Notes

Ground A appears before div. A1 only; ground B appears after div. A1 only. Source 2 is in score format. Order of divs. follows source 1; source 2 has A, A1–7, B, B1–7. A fermata appears at the end of each strain. M. 55, notes 5–7, slur in source 1 only. M. 104, L, editorial note is added to make multiple stop playable in standard tuning (see also no. 9, m. 10). M. 128, L, note 2, edition assumes bass clef as in source 2.

11. [DIVISIONS IN F MAJOR]

Source

GB:DRc, Mus MS. D.10, 149: "H: B:"

Notes

Ground appears on a separate staff below div. 1 and mm. 34–35 only. M. 15, note 8 lacks dots. M. 16, meter signature is ₵.

12. [DIVISIONS IN F MAJOR/D MINOR]

Source

GB:DRc, Mus MS. D.10, 150–51: "H: B"

Notes

Ground appears on a separate staff below div. 1 and m. 49 only. M. 13, L, note 1 also includes f♯. M. 15, U, notes 3 and 4, separated by extraneous sixteenth note (d'). M. 21, notes 9–12, slur includes note 8. M. 22,

note 6, d' is quarter note. M. 26, L, note 3, chord is G–d–f–a. M. 28, note 5 is sixteenth note. M. 31, U, notes 16, 18, and 20 have sharp. M. 39, U, note 4, double stop is b♭–f.

13. [DIVISIONS IN G MAJOR]

Source

GB:DRc, Mus MS. D.10, 156–59: "H. B."

Notes

Ground appears on a separate staff below divs. 1 and 16 only. M. 33, U, notes 1–3, edition assumes alto clef. M. 37, L, note 3 also appears to include an a', note 4 has dot. M. 46, note 7, sharp is placed before d'. M. 52, note 7 is c♯. M. 60, L, note 2 is f. Mm. 97–102 (U, note 3), edition assumes alto clef. M. 97, L, note 1, notated three times, in two clefs, only once with tie. M. 103, U, note 3, pitch is ambiguous—f' and g' also appear to be notated but with smaller noteheads. M. 129, note 4 is chord G–e–g–b.

14. [DIVISIONS IN A MINOR]

Sources

1. GB:Ob, MS. Mus. Sch. C.71, 106–8
2. GB:DRc, Mus MS. D.10, 94–97: "Búttler."
3. GB:DRc, Mus MS. D.10, 112–15: "H. B."
4. US:NYp, Drexel 3551, MS, 6–8: "Mr Henry Buttler."

Editions

Erslev, "Divisions," 105–13 (based on source 4); Richards, "Music for Bass Viol" 2:157–58 (based on sources 2 and 3).

Notes

Ground appears before div. 1 only; sources 2 and 3 are in score format. M. 12, L, notes 1–2 have slur in sources 3 and 4. M. 14, notes 1–2 and 3–4 have slur in sources 3 and 4. M. 20, L, notes 7 and 8 have sharp in sources 2, 3, and 4. M. 24, note 7 has sharp in sources 2, 3, and 4. M. 28, L, note 8, b is quarter note—edition follows sources 2, 3, and 4. M. 29, U, note 5, b is quarter note—edition follows sources 2, 3, and 4. M. 36, L, notes 15 and 16 have sharp in sources 2, 3, and 4. M. 40, U, note 11 has sharp in sources 2 and 4, note 20 is missing in source 2; L, note 2 is missing in source 2. M. 57, meter signature is $\frac{6}{1}$, with $\frac{6}{4}$ indicated in the margin following m. 56—edition follows sources 2 and 3. M. 60, U, note 1, editorial note added after sources 2, 3, and 4; L, note 1 is a—edition follows sources 2, 3, and 4. M. 69, U, note 4 is a'—edition follows sources 2, 3, and 4. M. 76, U, note 6 has sharp in sources 2, 3, and 4. M. 82, U, note 5 lacks one dot—edition follows source 4; L, note 3 has dot—edition follows source 4. M. 83, L, notes 3–4 have slur in sources 2, 3, and 4. M. 84, note 5, g♯ has dot—edition follows sources 2, 3, and 4.   M. 89, L, note 1 lacks stem.   Mm. 97–112 appear in source 1 only.   M. 109, U, notes 2–7, fingering numerals appear above notes.

15. [Divisions in A Minor]

Source

GB:DRc, Mus MS. D.10, 108–11: "H: B."

Notes

Ground appears on a separate staff below div. 8 only.   M. 35, L, note 1, A lacks dot.   M. 46, U, note 1, f' lacks dot.   M. 51, note 5, c' lacks dot.   M. 61, L, note 1, edition assumes bass clef.   M. 62, U, notes 5–7 are b♭', f', and c♯".   M. 69, edition assumes alto clef.   M. 72, U, note 2 has dot, notes 3 and 4, separated by extraneous quarter-note double stop (d'–g').   M. 78, L, note 4, A is quarter note.   M. 80, notes 7 and 9, c♯ and d are quarter notes.   M. 82, note 13 is eighth note.   M. 83, U, notes 1–4 are sixteenth notes, note 5 is eighth note; L, note 1 is eighth note.   M. 88, L, notes 3–6 are c, B, A, G.   M. 91, L, note 1, editorial note added to make multiple stop playable.   M. 97, L, note 3 is quarter note.   M. 98, note 4 is quarter note.   M. 104, note 6 is double stop c'–e♯'.   M. 109, L, notes 1–5, edition assumes bass clef.   M. 112, edition assumes alto clef for U, note 13, and L, note 2; U, note 13 lacks dot; L, note 2 lacks dots and sharp is placed before a.   M. 114, notes 2–7 are sixteenth notes.   M. 120, U, note 14 is double stop f'–a'.

16. [Sonata in E Minor]

Source

GB:DRc, Mus MS. D.10, 160–61: "H. B."

Notes

Number 16 immediately follows no. 7; both are in score format. Key signature of F-sharp is missing for mm. 9–35 (v and bc), 41–88 (v), and 66–88 (bc); all F-sharps in these measures are editorial, and all editorially marked F-naturals appear unsigned in the source.   Mm. 2–4, editorial notes added in conformity with mm. 5, 6, 8–10.   M. 6, note 1 is dotted eighth note, notes 6 and 7, separated by extraneous thirty-second notes (b", a").   Mm. 16–22, bc, alto clef.   M. 21, U, note 1, g' lacks dot.   M. 34, U, note 4 also appears to include b'; L, double stop B–d.   Mm. 36–82, most quarter notes are indicated by open-headed eighth notes, and all eighth notes by open-headed sixteenth notes (white notation); barlines group three, six, or nine half notes.   M. 44, L, note lacks dots.   M. 45, bc, note 2 (through m. 63), alto clef.   M. 48, bc, note 1 is chord g♯–d'–e'.   M. 49, bc, note 2 is tied to dot beginning m. 50.   Mm. 53–54, bc, notes lack dot.   M. 75, U and L, note 2, chord also includes whole note e.

17. Aria [in E Minor]

Sources

1. GB:DRc, Mus MS. D.2, 29 (vn), 31 (v), 35 (bc): "Aria"

2. GB:DRc, Mus MS. D.10, 218: "Aria"; "H Butler"

Notes

Source 1 consists of partbooks; source 2 is in score format.   M. 1, bc (through m. 5, note 2), alto clef.   M. 3, vn, note 5, ornament sign is // in source 2.   M. 4, v, note 8 is g' in both sources.   M. 5, bc, notes 4–5 are eighth notes in both sources.   M. 6, bc, note 3 is d♯ in both sources.   M. 8, bc, note 3 is B in both sources.   Mm. 9–10, repeat sign (:‖:) in source 2.   M. 14, v, note 7 (through m. 15, note 4), lacks key signature of F-sharp; bc, note 5 has ♯ as figure.   M. 15, v, note 7, quarter note is e in both sources.   M. 18, repeat sign (:‖: [*sic*]) at end in source 2; bc, note 3, figures are $^{6 5}_{4 \sharp}$.

18. Sonata [in F Major]

Sources

1. GB:DRc, Mus MS. D.2, 31 (vn), 33 (v), 27 (bc): "Sonata 21. a 2. viol: & viola."; "Butler"

2. B:Bc, MS. Litt. XY, no. 24.910, 56v–57r (vn), 56v–57r (v), 51v (bc): "Butler"

3. GB:DRc, Mus MS. D.5, 1 (vn), 1 (v), 1 (bc): "Sonata a 2. violino e viola"; "H. Butler"

4. GB:DRc, Mus MS. D.10, 212–14: "Fantasia à 2. Violino è Viola di G. del Sing.ʳ H[ein]rich Botler"; "H Bútler"

5. GB:HAdolmetsch, MS. II.C.25, 11r (vn), 11r (v), 9r (bc): "Sonata. 13. A. 2. Violino et viol de Gamba"; "H. Butler." (v), "Hen. Butler." (bc)

6. GB:Lgc, Gresham Mus. MS. 369, 95r (inverted, vn only): "Sonata"; "Butler"

7. GB:Ob, MS. Mus. Sch. C.71, 98–99 (v only)

8. GB:Ob, MS. Mus. Sch. D.249, 86r (vn), 87r (v), 91r (bc): "Sonata's a viola di gamba et violino"

Notes

Key signature of B-flat is missing for mm. 56–57 (bc) and 63–70 (bc); all affected notes in these measures are unsigned in source 1.   M. 6, v, note 1, c' appears below note 2 in m. 5—edition follows source 4.   M. 9, v, note 1, half note is g♯—edition follows sources 2, 3, 4, 5, and 7.   M. 15, bc, note 2 (through m. 18, note 2), alto clef.   M. 18, bc, note 1 is c, note 2 is illegible—in both cases edition follows sources 3, 4, and 5.   M. 20, v, notes 5–6 are c', c—edition follows sources 3 and 7.   Mm. 20–21, repeat sign (:‖:) in source 3 (all parts).   M. 22, v, note 2, b has natural (sharp) sign in sources 3, 4, and 7; bc, note 2 has figure 4♯—edition follows source 3.   M. 26, tempo indication from m. 28, bc, note 2.   M. 34, bc, note 2, *sic* all sources.   M. 36, v, note 2, b has natural (sharp) in sources 3, 4, and 7.   Mm. 38–39, repeat sign (:‖:) in sources 3 (all parts), 4, and 7 (v only).   M. 48, v, note 1 is illegible—edition follows sources 2, 3, 4, 5, 7, and 8. M. 52, v, second highest note of chord is d—edition follows sources 3, 4, 5, 7, and 8. Mm. 52–53, repeat sign (:‖:) in sources 1 (bc only), 3 (all parts), 4, 5 (bc only), and 7 (v only). M. 55, bc, note 1, bass clef. M. 60, v, note 4, f is illegible—edition follows sources 3, 5, and 7. M. 71, v, note 3, d appears below note 4—edition follows sources 2, 3, and 5. M. 72, v, note 1, bottom three notes lack stem. M. 73, repeat sign (:‖:) at end in sources 3 (vn only), 4, and 5 (all parts).

19. Sonata [in G Major]

Sources

1. GB:DRc, Mus MS. D.2, 28–29 (vn), 30–31 (v), 34 (bc): "Sonata 20. a 2. violi et viola"; "B5t*ℓ*2" (vn, v), "Buttler" (bc)

2. GB:DRc, Mus MS. D.5, 14–15 (vn), 14–15 (v), 14–15 (bc): "8 Sonata a 2. violino et viola"; "H Butler."

3. GB:DRc, Mus MS. D.10, 215–17: "Fantasia. à. 2. Violino. è Viola di G: del Sing.ʳ Heinrich Butler"; "H Butler"

Notes

Ornament signs are not placed precisely or uniformly in mm. 37–50 (vn and v); source 2 uses +, source 3 *tr* and //. The placement of the trill sign has been regularized in the edition. M. 1, vn, no tempo indication. M. 10, tempo indication from m. 14, v. M. 12, vn, note 5 has sharp in source 3. M. 13, vn, note 7 has sharp in sources 2 and 3. M. 27, vn, note 5 has sharp in source 3. M. 29, v, note 5 has sharp in source 3. M. 36, bc, marked *Soli*. M. 44, vn, note 5 has sharp in source 2. M. 50, v, note 7 has sharp in source 2. M. 59, v, editorial rest is confirmed in sources 2 and 3. M. 60, v, note 1 is half note—edition follows sources 2 and 3. M. 63, vn, meter signature is $\frac{4}{3}$; v and bc, meter signature is $\frac{3}{2}$. M. 81, v, note 8 has sharp in source 2. M. 91, bc, note 3, figure is 4♯. M. 98, v, note 2, chord is e–b–e′—edition follows source 2.

20. Sonata [in G Minor]

Sources

1. GB:DRc, Mus MS. D.2, 42–43 (vn), 44–45 (v), 38–39 (bc): "Sonata 28. a 2. violi et viola"; "B5t*ℓ*2" (v), "B" (vn, bc)

2. GB:DRc, Mus MS. D.5, 4–5 (vn), 4–5 (v), 4–5 (bc): "3 Sonata a 2. violino e viola"; "Zamponi"

3. GB:DRc, Mus MS. D.10, 219–22: "Sonata. à 2. Violino. è Viola di gamba Author Sing.ʳ"

4. GB:Lgc, Gresham Mus. MS. 369, 91r–90v (inverted, vn only): "Sonata"

Notes

M. 1, v, no tempo indication. M. 10, bc, note 6, sharp above note, not on staff. M. 14, bc, note 2, first figure is ♭. M. 20, vn, note 3 is g′—edition follows source 2. M. 22, tempo indication from vn, m. 26 (no tempo indication in v). M. 29, vn, note 5 has natural (sharp) sign in source 2. M. 30, v, note 6 has sharp in sources 2 and 3. M. 36, vn, note 5 has natural (sharp) sign in source 3. M. 37, vn, note 5 has sharp in source 2. M. 44, vn, note 3 has sharp in sources 2 and 3. M. 49, bc, note 2 has figure 6 above note—edition follows source 2. M. 58, vn, note 1 (through m. 59, note 1), half note, lacks dot—edition follows sources 2, 3, and 4. M. 72, bc, note 3, sharp is placed before note 4—edition follows source 2. M. 78, bc, note 3, figure is 4♯—edition follows source 2. M. 87, v, notes 1 and 2 are double stop d′–f′—edition follows source 2. M. 90, v, note 3 has sharp in source 2. M. 93, v, note 7 has sharp in source 2. Mm. 109–10, bc has two breves, not tied.

Acknowledgments

Numerous scholars, librarians, teachers, and performers have contributed to the preparation of this volume and the dissertation that preceded it. I am extremely grateful to them all. Financial support was provided by a Nussbaum Fellowship for research abroad, awarded by the Department of Music, Washington University in St. Louis, and also by a Faculty Research Grant from West Georgia College.

I acknowledge with deep gratitude the many libraries in which I studied and the assistance of their staffs. For providing access to documents and microfilms used for this volume, I especially thank the Dean and Chapter Library, Durham; the Bodleian Library, Oxford; the Royal College of Music, London; the Guildhall Library, London; the Dolmetsch Library, Haslemere; the Music Division, The New York Public Library, Astor, Lenox, & Tilden Foundations; the Bibliothèque du Conservatoire Royal de Musique, Brussels; and the Archivo General de Palacio, Madrid.

Lila Aamodt and Aaron Appelstein of A-R Editions deserve credit for many improvements to this edition. Jack Ashworth proved an invaluable collaborator, and I am indebted to him for far more than his excellent commentary and realizations.

Elizabeth V. Phillips

Notes

1. Elizabeth Van Vorst Phillips, "The Divisions and Sonatas of Henry Butler" (Ph.D. diss., Washington University in St. Louis, 1982), provides a more detailed biography of Butler and discussion of his music.

2. Madrid, Archivo General de Palacio, Sección Administrativa: Capilla, legajos 1115, 1135, 1137; Casa, Vestuarios, legajo 973; Casa, Mercedes, raciones, gajes, legajo 866; Expedientes personales, cajas 137/20, 150/4. Most of these documents are cited by José Subirá, "Dos músicos del Rey Felipe IV: B. Jovenardi y E. Butler," *Anuario musical* 19 (1964): 201–23; I am indebted to Louise K. Stein for bringing one document to my attention.

3. James Wadsworth, *The English Spanish Pilgrime; or, A New Discoverie . . . with the Estate of the English Pentioners and Fugitiues under the King of "Spaines Dominions". . .* (London: T. C. for Michael Sparke, 1629), 63.

4. These works, for two treble instruments, bass string instrument, and basso continuo, appear in Andrea Falconieri, *Il primo libro di canzone* (Naples: Pietro Paolini e Giuseppe Ricci, 1650; facsm. repr. Florence: Studio per Edizione Scelte, 1980), 23–24 (canto), 23–24 (altro canto), 21–22 (basso), 21–22 (basso continuo).

5. Christopher Simpson, *The Division-Violist; or, An Introduction to the Playing upon a Ground* (London: William Godbid, 1659), 47–48.

6. Jean Rousseau, *Traité de la viole* (Paris: Christophe Ballard, 1687; repr. Amsterdam: Antiqua, 1965), 17–18.

7. The royal palace in Madrid burned in 1734, destroying the library of the Capilla Real; see José García Marcellán, *Catálogo del archivo de música de la real capilla de palacio* (Madrid: Editorial del Patrimonio Nacional, [1938]), 9.

8. Simpson, *The Division-Violist*. The publication was revised and issued as *Chelys Minuritionum. . . . The Division-Viol; or, The Art of Playing "Ex tempore" upon a Ground*, 2d ed. (London: W. Godbid for Henry Brome, 1665; on some copies the date is changed to 1667); this edition was reissued (London: William Pearson for Richard Mears and Allexander Livingston, 1712).

9. A set of divisions in D minor, found in twelve sources and most often attributed to Polewheele, bears Butler's name in one source. The work is not included in the present edition. Regarding attribution of this work and of number 8, see Phillips, "Divisions and Sonatas," 69–76.

10. Butler's ground bass models are noted by Veronika Gutmann, *Die Improvisation auf der Viola da gamba in England im 17. Jahrhundert und ihre Wurzeln im 16. Jahrhundert*, Wiener Veröffentlichungen zur Musikwissenschaft, vol. 19 (Tutzing: Hans Schneider, 1979), 220–24.

11. Simpson's term; *The Division-Violist*, 45.

12. An anonymous, incomplete prelude-divisions pair exists in London, Library of the Royal College of Music [hereafter GB:Lcm] II.F.10(2.). A work by William Young (see n. 15), found in the same manuscript, comprises Prelude, Divisions, and Triple. No other prelude-sonata pair is known to the editor.

13. The E-minor sonata (no. 16) is discussed in Elizabeth V. Phillips, "Henry Butler and the Early Viol Sonata," *Journal of the Viola da Gamba Society of America* 21 (1984): 45–52.

14. In his edition of the Sonata in G Minor (Purcell's only "solo" sonata), Thurston Dart speculates that a missing *concertante* bass part would make this work a sonata *a 2*; see Henry Purcell, *Fantazias and Other Instrumental Music*, ed. Thurston Dart, The Works of Henry Purcell, vol. 31 (London: Novello, 1959), 95–100, 112.

15. Probably the composer of sonatas published in Innsbruck in 1653. Another William Young served the English court from 1660 to 1670; I am grateful to David Lasocki for information regarding the latter. See also n. 12 above.

16. This composer remains to be identified; relevant manuscripts include the names "Anthony Poole," "F. Poole," and "P. Poul."

17. The term *sett* was used by Roger North, *Roger North on Music: Being a Selection from His Essays Written during the Years c. 1695–1728*, ed. John Wilson (London: Novello, 1959), 295.

18. Regarding the attribution of number 20, see Phillips, "Divisions and Sonatas," 101–3. Gioseffo Zamponi, an Italian contemporary of Butler, left two trio sonatas for violins and continuo, which appear simpler in style than number 20. Although Zamponi is not known to have composed for viol, his possible authorship of number 20 cannot be entirely discounted.

19. Regarding string instruments, see Stephen Bonta, "Terminology for the Bass Violin in Seventeenth-Century Italy," *Journal of the American Musical Instrument Society* 4 (1978): 5–42.

20. See Michael Tilmouth, "The Sources of Chamber Music in England, 1675–1720," 2 vols. (Ph.D. diss., Cambridge University, 1960), 1:274; Peter Evans, "Seventeenth-Century Chamber Music Manuscripts at Durham," *Music and Letters* 36 (1955): 205, 212, 216; Jane T. Johnson, "The English Fantasia-Suite, ca. 1620–1660" (Ph.D. diss., University of California, Berkeley, 1971), 285, 388–91; Ruth Halle Rowen, *Early Chamber Music*, 2d ed. (New York: Da Capo Press, 1974), 84–85; Jane T. Johnson, correspondence, *Early Music* 6 (July 1978): 481; Peter Holman, correspondence, *Early Music* 6 (July 1978): 482–83; Ernst H. Meyer, *Early English Chamber Music: From the Middle Ages to Purcell*, 2d rev. ed. (London: Lawrence and Wishart, 1982), 241–45.

21. This tuning is not one of the fifty-five listed by Gordon Dodd in his *Thematic Index of Music for Viols* (London: Viola da Gamba Society, 1980–89), p. TUN-1.

22. Butler's use of tempo indications resembles that of his Italian contemporaries, for example, Dario Castello, regarding whose tempos, see Eleanor Selfridge-Field's preface to her edition of Castello, *Selected Ensemble Sonatas*, pt. 1, Recent Researches in the Music of the Baroque Era, vol. 23 (Madison: A-R Editions, 1977), x–xi. A more extensive discussion of seventeenth-century meter and tempo appears in George Houle, *Meter in Music, 1600–1800: Performance, Perception, and Notation* (Bloomington: Indiana University Press, 1987), chap. 1.

23. *The New Grove Dictionary of Music and Musicians*, s.v. "Presto," by David Fallows.

24. Regarding Italian ornamentation in the early seventeenth century, see Selfridge-Field's preface to Castello, *Sonatas*, xi–xii; see also Stewart Carter, "On the Shape of the Early Baroque Trill," *Historical Performance* 3, no. 1 (Spring 1990): 9–17, for examples of the *trillo* and *tremolo*.

25. Some of Butler's works have appeared in modern editions: numbers 1, 8, and 14, in Janet M. Richards, "A Study of Music for Bass Viol Written in England in the Seventeenth Century," 3 vols. (B.Litt. thesis, University of Oxford, 1961), 2:153–58, 182–83; numbers 2, 4, and 8, in Gutmann, *Die Improvisation*, app., 9–16; numbers 2, 7–10, and 14, in Wendy Erslev, "Divisions to a Ground (*Drexel 3551*): An Edition and

Commentary" (Master's thesis, Brooklyn College, 1977), 105–13, 136–46, 178–89, 195–205.

26. For further description of the sources, see Phillips, "Divisions and Sonatas," 134–38.

27. See nn. 5 and 8 above.

28. Andrew Ashbee suggests sharing of manuscripts in "The Four-Part Instrumental Compositions of John Jenkins," 3 vols. (Ph.D. diss., London University, 1966), 1:29.

29. Simpson, *The Division-Violist*, 49–50.

30. The *Thematic Index* entry for Butler also includes Falconieri's "Canciona" and "Su gallarda" dedicated to Butler, the divisions attributed to Polewheele (see n. 9 above), and two works by Orlando Gibbons erroneously attributed to Butler in one manuscript.

31. Simpson, *The Division-Violist*, 47.

Commentary on the
Basso Continuo Realizations

Sources

Since Henry Butler spent the bulk of his adult life in Spain, it would be proper to include Spanish continuo sources among the treatises consulted. Yet the Spanish did not concern themselves overmuch with continuo theorizing: in the handlist of continuo sources compiled by Peter Williams in his *Figured Bass Accompaniment*,[1] there is but one source describing continuo practice from a Spanish pen, an eighteenth-century treatise by Joseph de Torres y Martinez Bravo (*Reglas generales de acompañar, en órgano, clavicordio y harpa* [Madrid: La Imprenta de Música, 1702]). The realizations for the present edition were written according to guidelines found in Italian, English, and German sources spanning the years 1607–74.

Texture

The texture of the keyboard realization varies freely from two to four voices. While four-voice accompaniments are frequently stipulated in continuo manuals of the seventeenth century, such instruction books and directions most often pertain to the accompaniment either of vocal and instrumental ensembles or of a solo voice. In either case a full, four-voice texture generally can be sustained over a long period with little danger of covering up the person(s) being accompanied, something less often possible when accompanying instrumental soloists. The present realizations are intentionally sparse for this reason, although players should feel free to add notes or rearrange chords as they feel necessary—only being sure that the continuo does not mask the solo part(s). For example, quick passages in the solo should be accompanied only by the simplest chords; the accompanist should not attempt to match the motion in the solo part.

The second section of number 16 begins imitatively. Concerning fugal entries Michael Praetorius, unlike later theorists, suggested that performers not double imitative entries note for note after the first point of imitation:

> If the piece begins with a point of imitation or a chorale [tune], then the organist should also begin the entry as it appears, with only one voice, or one key; however, when the other voices join in afterward, he is free to add more keys according to what pleases him.[2]

To preserve balance the editorial part in number 16 constitutes a single-line accompaniment matching the contour of the solo part without doubling it (see mm. 18–23).

Unfigured Basses

All but four of Butler's pieces are unfigured, and the realizations reflect period instructions for supplying appropriate harmonies. For example, ascending motion by half step in the bass generally suggests that the chord over the first note be what we would call a first-inversion triad, the chord over the second a root-position triad. Matthew Locke explains: "On the *half-Note* below the *Tone* you play in, on the Third and Sixt *Major* above the *Tone*, on B *sharp* (when E is not the *Tone*) and on all *sharp Notes* out of the *Tone*, Play a *Sixth Minor* except the rule of *Cadences* take place."[3]

Players who opt to improvise realizations rather than to use those supplied should be aware that in the division sets the harmony of the solo part occasionally requires adjustment in the accompaniment from one statement of the ground to the next. For example, the continuo player may need to substitute a first-inversion chord for what had been a root-position triad, or shift from major to minor or vice versa.

In pieces where figures occur, one must also consider the precise import of those figures and how they relate to the texture of the realization. Are the figures to be taken as prescriptions, requiring one to play a note corresponding to every interval suggested by the figure? Or do some of the figures act merely as reporters, advising the continuo player of which harmonies to expect at any given note, harmonies that are present in any case in the upper parts and that need not be doubled by the continuo player? Practical experience suggests the latter; in many cases, if all intervals of a figure are supplied by the continuo player, especially on an organ, the soloist(s) may be completely overpowered.

Choice of Continuo Instrument

The standard choice of continuo instrument for chamber music in seventeenth-century England was the chamber organ; indeed, the use of plucked keyboard instruments is rarely suggested there before the middle of the seventeenth century. Although the harpsichord is mentioned in conjunction with what we might consider a chamber ensemble as early as 1607 (see Thomas Campion, *The Discription* [sic] *of a Maske . . . in Honour of the Lord Hayes*), reference to the harpsichord is found only four times on English title pages through 1632: Tobias Hume's *Poeticall Musicke* (1607), Martin Peerson's *Private Musicke* (1620), Peerson's *Mottects; or, Grave Chamber Musique* (1630), and Walter Porter's Italianate *Madrigales and Ayres* (1632). Porter uses the term "harpesechord"; the other references are to "virginals." And the wording of Peerson's 1630 preface may be significant: "For want of organs, [the Mottects] may be performed on Virginals, Base-Lute, Bandora, or Irish Harpe." Clearly, the harpsichord is not the instrument of choice.

Thomas Mace suggests that the choice between harpsichord and organ depends on the music being performed:

> We had for our *Grave Musick, Fancies* of 3, 4, 5, and 6 *Parts* to the *Organ;* Interpos'd (now and then) with some *Pavins, Allmaines, Solemn,* and *Sweet Delightful Ayres.* . . .
> And *These Things* were *Performed,* upon so many *Equal, and Truly-Sciz'd Viols;* . . . The *Organ Evenly, Softly, and Sweetly Acchording to All.* . . .
> But when we would be most *Ayrey, Jocond, Lively,* and *Spruce;* Then we had *Choice,* and *Singular Consorts,* either for 2, 3, or 4 *Parts,* but not to the *Organ* (as many (now a days) *Improperly,* and *Unadvisedly* perform such like *Consorts* with) but to the *Harpsicon;* yet more *Properly,* and much better to the *Pedal.* . . .[4]

A typical English chamber organ of 1620–50 would have been a small instrument with either no pedal or, at most, a few pedal keys connected by "hook-downs" to corresponding manual notes. When playing the present accompaniments on a modern organ, one will almost certainly need to limit the choice of stops to one 8' flute in order to preserve balance with the string instrument(s). The pedal should be either avoided entirely or coupled to the manual with no 16' drawn.

Accompanying Division Sets

Thirteen pieces in the present volume are sets of divisions, where the accompaniment is based on a ground bass. Should the accompanist play the same accompaniment over and over again, or should he or she join in the display of improvisatory (and technical) bravura? Later writers such as St. Lambert (1707) and C. P. E. Bach (1753, 1762) inveigh specifically against an unseemly display of keyboard virtuosity. For that matter, it is virtually impossible for a keyboard player to match up quick notes with a soloist; the attempt makes for very sloppy ensemble playing. Christopher Simpson suggests that when two viols and keyboard are used to improvise divisions, the players should take turns:

> When the *Viols* have thus (as it were) Vied and Revied one to the other, *A.* ['him who Plays upon the *Organ* or *Harpsechord';* later, '*Organist*'] if he have ability of Hand, may, upon a sign given him, put in his Strain of *Division;* the two *Viols* Playing one of them the *Ground,* and the other *slow* Descant to it. *A.* having finished his Strain, a reply thereto may be made, first by one *Viol,* and then by the other.[5]

In the present pieces the viol is making divisions virtually all of the time, and so the accompanist must be content to play the simplest accompaniments, varying only to accommodate changes in harmony or to shift register or add motion in response to the viol part. Otherwise, each accompaniment is to be heard as a point of stability, against which the divisions themselves are a source of contrast. Exceptions might occur in places where the viol has "*slow* Descant," such as the first division of number 13. The keyboard player could create a more elaborate part here, if the viol player does not add ornamentation.

Jack Ashworth

Notes

1. Peter Williams, *Figured Bass Accompaniment,* 2 vols. (Edinburgh: University of Edinburgh Press, 1970). This is one of two standard general works on continuo accompaniment, the other being F. T. Arnold's *Art of Accompaniment from a Thorough-Bass As Practised in the XVIIth & XVIIIth Centuries* (London: Oxford University Press, 1931).

2. "Wenn der Gesang von einer *Fugen* oder *Choral* ansehet/so sol der Organist auch also nur mit einer Stimme oder Griff uff einem *Clave* oder *Calculo,* die *Fugam* wie sie gesetzt ist/anfangen: Wenn aber hernacher die andere Stimmen darzu kommen/so stehets ihm frey/mehr *Claves* nach seinem guten gefallen darzu zugreiffen." Michael Praetorius, *Syntagma Musicum,* vol. 3 (Wolfenbüttel: Elias Holwein, 1619; facsm. repr. Kassel: Bärenreiter, 1959), 138. The translation is mine. "Calculo" (piece of ivory) is here roughly equivalent to "key."

3. Matthew Locke, *Melothesia; or, Certain General Rules for Playing upon a Continued-Bass* (London: J. Carr, 1673), cited in Arnold, *Art of Accompaniment,* 155.

4. Thomas Mace, *Musick's Monument; or, A Remembrancer of the Best Practical Musick* (London: by T. Ratcliffe and N. Thompson for the author, 1676; facsm. repr., 2 vols., ed. J. Jacquot and A. Souris, Paris: Editions du Centre National de la Recherche Scientifique, 1966), 1:234–35. Although Mace published in 1676, he wrote of the practices in vogue in his "Younger Time" (1:233).

5. Christopher Simpson, *Chelys Minuritionum. . . . The Division-Viol; or, The Art of Playing "Ex tempore" upon a Ground,* 2d ed. (London: W. Godbid for Henry Brome, 1665/67; facsm. repr. London: J. Curwen & Sons, 1955), 58.

Plate 1. Henry Butler, [Prelude in E Minor] (no. 7 in the edition), and beginning of [Sonata in E Minor] (no. 16 in the edition), for bass viol and basso continuo. Durham, Cathedral, Dean and Chapter Library, Mus MS. D.10, 160 (source dimensions: 115 × 230 mm). Reproduced by permission.

Plate 2. Henry Butler, continuation of [Sonata in E Minor] (no. 16 in the edition), for bass viol and basso continuo. Durham, Cathedral, Dean and Chapter Library, Mus MS. D.10, 161 (source dimensions: 115 × 230 mm). Reproduced by permission.

Plate 3. Henry Butler, Sonata [in F Major] (no. 18 in the edition), for violin, bass viol, and basso continuo. Durham, Cathedral, Dean and Chapter Library, Mus MS. D.2, violin partbook, 31 (source dimensions: 312 × 204 mm). Reproduced by permission.

1. [Divisions in C Major]

*[Bass viol]

[Basso
continuo]

* Tune lowest string to C.

2. [Divisions in C Major]

* Tune lowest string to C.

3. [Divisions in C Major]

4. [Divisions in D Major]

5. [Divisions in D Minor]

6. [Divisions in D Minor]

7. [Prelude in E Minor]

8. [Divisions in E Minor]

9. [Prelude in F Major]

[Bass viol]

[Basso continuo]

10. [Divisions in F Major]

11. [Divisions in F Major]

12. [Divisions in F Major/D Minor]

13. [Divisions in G Major]

14. [Divisions in A Minor]

15. [Divisions in A Minor]

16. [Sonata in E Minor]

[Bass viol]

[Basso continuo]

17. Aria [in E Minor]

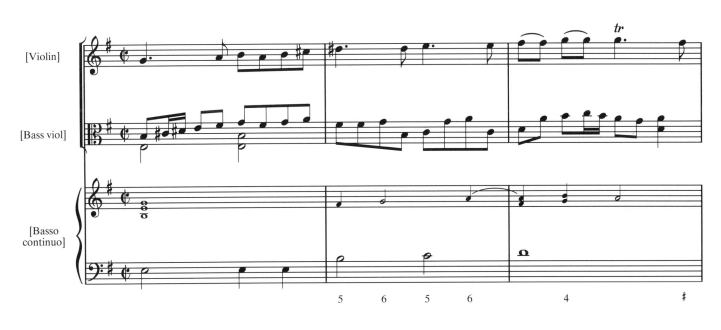

18. Sonata [in F Major]

19. Sonata [in G Major]

20. Sonata [in G Minor]